Blanket

Row 1 (RS): With larger hook and CC, work **first foundation hdc** (see Stitch Tutorial on page 2), work 59 **next foundation hdc** (see Stitch Tutorial), **change to MC** (see Pattern Notes and Stitch Tutorial), work 60 next foundation half double crochet, turn. *(120 hdc)*

Row 2: With smaller hook, **ch 1** (see Pattern Notes), work **beg khdc** (see Stitch Tutorial), work 59 **next khdc** (see Stitch Tutorial), change to CC, work 59 next khdc, work **last khdc** (see Stitch Tutorial), turn. *(120 khdc)*

Row 3: Ch 1, work beg khdc, work 59 next khdc, change to CC, work 59 next khdc, work last khdc, turn.

Rows 4–21: Rep rows 2 and 3.

Row 22: Rep row 2.

Row 23: Ch 1, following **Chart** (see Pattern Notes and Chart) work beg khdc, work 32 next khdc, change to MC, work 3 next khdc, change to CC, work 24 next khdc, change to MC, work 1 next khdc, change to CC, work 7 next khdc, change to MC, work 51 khdc, work last khdc, turn.

Rows 24–130: Work as established, following Chart for color changes.

Fasten off. ●

KEY	
■	MC
□	CC

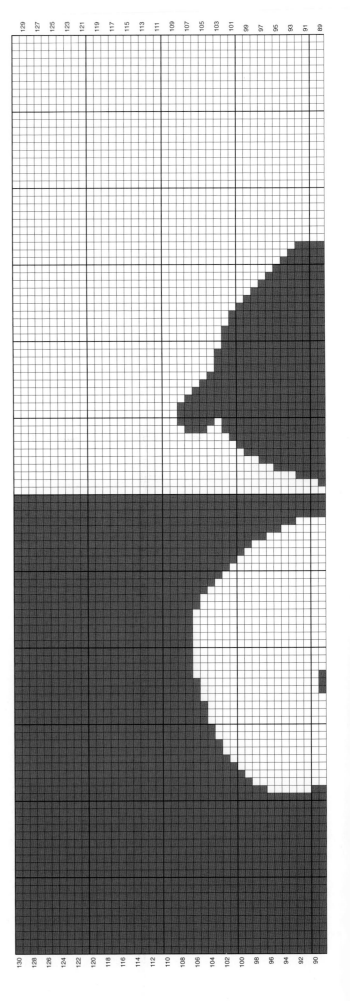

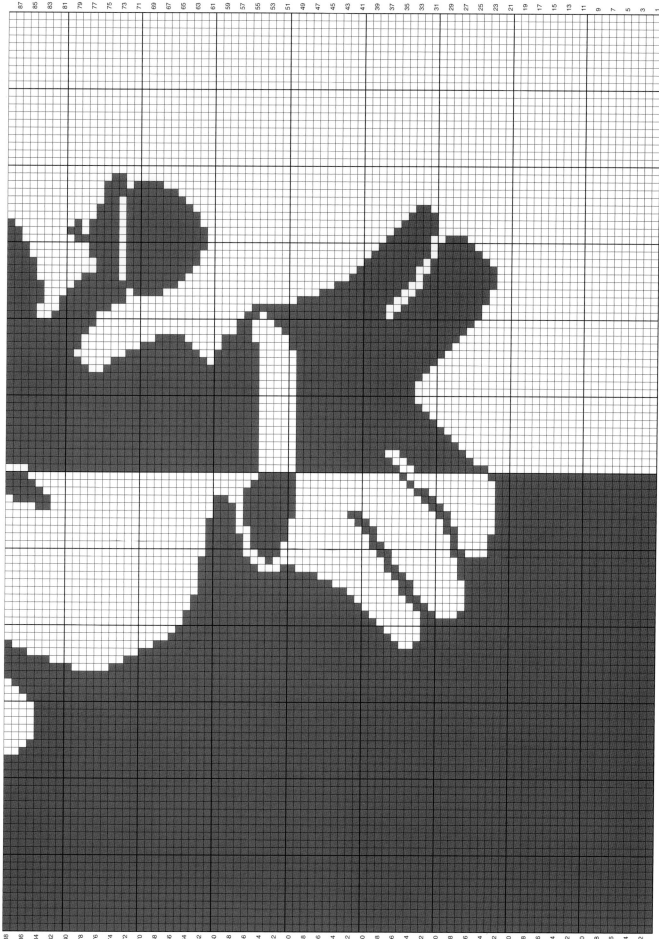

Feeling Squirrelly Blanket
Chart

Sam Buck

Tales From The Reef

AuthorHouse™ UK
1663 Liberty Drive
Bloomington, IN 47403 USA
www.authorhouse.co.uk
UK TFN: 0800 0148641 (Toll Free inside the UK)
UK Local: 02036 956322 (+44 20 3695 6322 from outside the UK)

Because of the dynamic nature of the Internet, any web addresses or
links contained in this book may have changed since publication and
may no longer be valid. The views expressed in this work are solely those
of the author and do not necessarily reflect the views of the publisher,
and the publisher hereby disclaims any responsibility for them.

Any people depicted in stock imagery provided by Getty Images are models,
and such images are being used for illustrative purposes only.
Certain stock imagery © Getty Images.

This book is printed on acid–free paper.

ISBN: 978–1–7283–5668–6 (sc)
ISBN: 978–1–7283–5667–9 (e)

Print information available on the last page.

Published by AuthorHouse 09/08/2020

author HOUSE®

Tales from the Reef: Contents

The Tale of Fifi the Flatfish

Fifi is a flatfish. Flatfish like Fifi live at the bottom of the sea and they look as if someone has taken a rolling pin over a much fatter fish and rolled it back and forth to make flatfish like Fifi.

Fifi, like all the flatfish in the ocean, is a rather drab pinky brown colour almost like the colour of the sand or mud on the sea floor.

She was also a little odd looking, very odd looking actually. I mean really odd looking.

There lay Fifi's trouble; she looked so strange, being so flat with big bubble eyes on top of her head, that all the other fish would avoid her and make fun of her or just be generally mean to her.

This always made Fifi very sad, although she would never give up trying to get involved in all the other games the rest of the fish were playing.

One day when Fifi woke up she saw the other fish swimming off together. "Where are you all going?" Fifi called after them.

"We're going off an adventure and we weren't planning on someone looking like you to come with us!" they all shouted back. "But if you can keep up with us we might just let you tag along" they laughed at her.

Fifi swam as hard as she could behind them

However when you're an odd shaped flatfish, swimming fast is not easily done.

She could just see them in the distance as they all swam into a clear area of the sea floor beyond the reef.

It was not a nice place. There were sunken ships littering the sea floor and many more passing over the surface making it quite a dark area!

The sharks were out and looking mean! The other fish swam in the wreck to investigate. Fifi thought it wiser to stay outside the wreck. This was a good idea. The sharks had seen the others and were not happy they were in their area. So the sharks chased them here and there and all of a sudden a fish trap fell from the surface...

Fifi was worried and with good reason. The sharks chased the other fish straight into the trap... and as you can no doubt guess, they were now well and truly trapped!!

"Help us someone!" they cried.

This was Fifi's moment... Using her shape and colour she was able to glide just above the sand of the sea floor completely unnoticed by the sharks and get to the trap. As she was able to slip in and out between the bars of the trap and pick the lock she got the rest of the fish out and free.

The next thing Fifi did was one of the bravest things you would ever see done by anyone...

She shouted to the sharks to come and get her if they could...

So they tried, but they could not see her or find her as she just kept on disappearing and blending in with the sea floor and so all the other fish escaped and got home safely!!

When Fifi eventually got home safely to she was greeted as the hero she was by all the other fish.

Do you know what she was always the best at hide and seek too, no one could ever find her.

The other fish learned a valuable lesson too. They learnt that they should never have judged Fifi on how she looked for even the oddest looking person can be the bravest one and also, especially in Fifi's case, can be the life and Sole of the party!!

The tale of Dizzy the Trumpet fish and the Domino the Whale

Desmond is a trumpet fish. Trumpet fish are long and thin with an oddly shaped nose; some are silver and some are gold. It's no wonder then that with an odd nose and the colour they're called Trumpet fish... They do look like trumpets (kind of!).

Don't let the name fool you though – there's hardly a trumpet fish out there that can actually play... Desmond is one of the exceptions, he actually wanted to play the trumpet... But there lay his problem. How was he going to learn properly and what type of music band should he join? It was time to go searching...

First of all Desmond tried out for the army band but the sergeant major fish said, "no" to him joining the fish army as he, "didn't have the right stuff".

Next he tried out for the choir... He thought surely that fish with voices like Angels (strangely also known as Angel Fish), would welcome him; however when Desmond started playing along with the singing it created a panic... Angels and trumpets are not a good mix!!

Then Desmond tried out for the sea circus but couldn't quite get the timing right and was laughed out of the ring by the clown fish. Desmond thought that was a bit mean. "Why don't you get lost," he said to one of the clown fish (that's a whole different story altogether though) as he swam away. He tried out for all the other fish groups he could think of... The Stonefish rock band, the pipe fish & blow fish woodwind band and the Guitar Shark group.

He couldn't make it work anywhere! Desmond took up busking on the reef, still determined to be heard, hoping some fish will hear him and like what they heard! Everyday he was out there playing away, with no luck. One day though, as he was trumpeting away, a dark shadow came over him and he heard a booming voice...

"Hey man, I'm Domino thejazz– singing whale. What tune are you trying to toot on the trumpet?"

"Hello Domino, I'm Desmond the trumpet fish. I don't really know what tune I'm playing. I've tried for so many different types of band that I have no real style and just end up going round in circles!!"

"Desmond my man, there's nothing wrong with trying out different things and styles, how else will you know what you're best suited too? Going round in circles though... That's just gonna make you dizzy.

Come to think of it I like that name for you. From now on, you're Dizzy the trumpet playing trumpet fish."

"I like the sound of that," said Desmond (sorry) said Dizzy.

"What am I supposed to do about my playing style though Domino?"

"Okay Dizzy, let me level with you... I kinda like your sound already... It's like jazz. Jazz has no fixed sound or style and you can make it up as you go along!"

Domino looked very seriously at Dizzy, then smiled.

"Dizzy, I would like you to come on tour with me. Together, with your unique jazz tunes and my voice, we'll be huge... Whaddya say?"

Dizzy was ecstatic. He'd made it after all and with someone he'd never expected to meet at all.

So Dizzy and Domino toured the oceans together, Dizzy playing and Domino singing... In fact, they're so good and successful that they're still going today. If you're in the right part of the ocean you can can hear Domino singing away... But don't forget he couldn't be that good a singer without his pal Dizzy.

It just goes to show that even the unlikeliest friendships and given the right mix, the sky's the limit (or in Domino and Dizzys case the ocean surface).

The Tail of Eight-fingered Edgar the Octopus and the Sonny the Sergeant Major Fish

Did you know that in the world there are many types of people. Most of them are good, some are bad, some start off good lose their way or get mixed up with the wrong people and can be naughty and others start as bad but then become good.

Let me tell you about Edgar the Octopus, he was all sorts of naughty.

Edgar was a genius, there was very little he couldn't do. Put him in a maze and he would find his way out super quick... In fact he could work his way out of almost any tight spot he found himself in.

He was also a master of disguise and, I'm very sad to say, a master burglar...

He could hide out anywhere on the reef without being seen and when the poor unsuspecting family turned their backs...

Edgar would pounce and everything in their home would be gone...

He had, as you might say, very sticky fingers (and I'm not just referring to the suckers on his arms). As I said, a very naughty Octopus he was.

The reef police, who were run by the Sergeant Major fish, were baffled by the mystery that Edgar's actions left behind... Apart from Sonny.

Sonny was new to the reef police and had his suspicions about Edgar.

So Sonny decided to follow Edgar, determined to catch him in the act. This turned out to be a lot harder than Sonny first thought. He stuck at it though, but he could never catch Edgar red handed, (really difficult when an octopus like Edgar can change colour at will!).

He did track him down to his hideout...quite a messy area, made to look that way to deter fish like Sonny from prying.

There was no Aladin's cave of stolen goods though — it was empty. But Sonny was amazed that, in the poorest part of the reef, the families had so much stuff!

Sonny confronted Edgar:

"I know it is you who's been stealing from lots of others, although it looks like all the stolen stuff has been passed on to the less fortunate... Still doesn't mean you don't have to pay for the crimes you have committed!" exclaimed Sonny.

Edgar replied, "But you have no proof that it was me. No one has seen me do anything wrong and even though these gifts to the poorer families are from me, you have no proof where they came from and it's also not as if I'm that stupid to confess anything to you either."

Sonny suddenly had a thought... He knew Edgar was responsible for the burglaries but tried a different approach...

"Edgar, what do you feel like when you take from others and does that compare with how you feel when you help the less fortunate?" Edgar was stunned by this. He had to admit that even though he was (or so he believed) only taking from those who could afford it, he still felt bad about it, whereas giving to others made him feel good.

So Sonny offered him a deal — join him and help do good for everyone not just the few and pay his debt back that way. Edgar agreed and from then on he used his skills to help and he was a happier Octopus for it. He took greater care of where he lived, built a garden and everything.

So no matter how bad or naughty someone may appear to be there is always a way back for them to be good, just like Edgar. To be honest with you I know where I'd like to be... I'd like to be under the sea in an Octopus's Garden like Edgar's.

The tale of Francesco the Monkfish and the Wolf fish

This story is an old one, it happened many, many years ago... long before you and I were born in fact. Life was different back then, everyone had different beliefs and faiths.

Take Francesco for example. Francesco was a Monkfish and as such he followed a simple life. Francesco had opted for a life of poverty, choosing to dedicate his life to teaching others about the wonders of the world and how lucky everyone was to be alive in such a paradise.

He also looked after all the sick fish and was famous throughout the reef for doing so.

Francesco was also a big believer in peace, but over the years there weren't many peaceful times (different fish believed different things and this wasn't good for peace!). Francesco began to lose his belief and faith in the goodness of the world. This was sad and Francesco started to turn his back on the good work he was doing as he thought it wasn't making any difference!

So Francesco turned away from his previous life with his faith and his belief shattered!

Even though times of peace returned to the reef Francesco still didn't return to what he used to be, until a very strange turn of events occurred.

One day there were rumours of a wolf fish running amok just outside of the reef.

The wolf fish was making so much trouble that all the other fish were too scared to go anywhere and the more scared they got the bolder the wolf fish got and the more trouble it would make.

The rest of the fish didn't know what to do. So they went to Francesco for help, but he wasn't interested.

"This is what happens when we ignore a life of peace for so long, it allows the bad parts of our world to take over and there's nothing I can do about it!"

The rest of the fish were distraught. They needed help but where was it going to come from?

One day, when Francesco was going about his business, he suddenly heard a very weird voice in his head...

"This is the Voice of Cod... I know you have lost your faith but all the fish need you to find it again somehow... All the work you used to do will help you sort out the troubles the reef are currently going through... Go out there with me in your heart and you will be able to get rid of the wolf fish... I believe and have faith in you!"

So, with renewed faith and belief, Francesco went out to face the wolf fish. His mind was so firmly set with the new confidence he had in himself it took him little time to turn the wolf fish away.

No one knows quite how he did it but after he had succeeded he felt reborn and renewed.

It just goes to show that, even those that have lost faith in themselves can be encouraged to find it again. Sometimes, a little belief in them, will make them able to perform miracles (or is it just the sheer power of Cod that does it... personally I'm not sure about that!)

The tale of how the Hammerhead Shark got its hammerhead

Many years ago, when all the fish and seas creatures were finding their places in the great order pf things, the sharks were all the same shape, but NOT all the same size. Some, like the Dwarf Lantern Shark, were teeny, tiny things while others were larger like the enormous whale shark (which, as its name suggests was as big as a whale, and that's BIG!). Some Sharks looked mean and scary and some looked soft and gentle. I wouldn't say they were cuddly though as, with skin like sandpaper, cuddling a shark is probably not the best thing to do.

So let's get back to the story. A long, long time ago the sharks were trying to decide which of them should be the first leader and king of their kind, but could they agree on anything? Of course they couldn't.

The Whale shark said, "I am the biggest and I swim the furthest around the oceans. I see more than you other sharks, so you should respect me. I should be your king and leader.

The Oceanic White Tip disagreed though. "I see as much as much as you on my long travels why shouldn't I be king?"

"I should be king" said the Great White shark. "I am the meanest and scariest of you all. I can keep you all in line because you fear me!"

However, the Tiger Shark and Sand Tiger Shark (or Ragged Tooth Shark) claimed that they too were equally mean and scary looking so why didn't they deserve to be chosen?

The Mako Shark joined in saying, "I am the fastest and most athletic, so I deserve to be king because I am naturally superior to all of you" to which the Blue Shark replied, "I am just as quick and agile as you!"

And so they continued without agreeing amongst themselves. Why should that be? Well you see, size is no measure of true greatness, as the bigger you are the harder you fall. Fear and meanness is also no quality of leadership, as such leaders succeed only in turning all other against them. Likewise, pride in being athletic will only make others try harder to get the better of you and they will do as pride always comes before a fall.

What then, could they do to decide who should be their king?
They decided to go and ask Big Blue, the wisest creature in
all the ocean.

Big Blue listened carefully to the Sharks question. "How do we choose who should be the first to be the king of the sharks.

Big Blue gave it some thought and then in a slow, melodic voice said, "As you all have such high opinions of yourselves you'll never be able to agree who leads you. A vote won't solve your problem either. I will set a test for you to see which of you is most worthy to lead. Leave me now and tomorrow you will have your test. The one and only shark who solves the problem and passes the test will be your first king.

The next morning, as good as her word, Big Blue left her test. In a clear patch of sand on the ocean floor was the biggest rock the sharks and fishes had ever seen.

Written on the enormous stone was a message:

"*The shark worthy enough to lead you and be king is the one who can move this rock and.......flip it over*"

All the sharks set about trying to move the rock. The Whale Shark tied seaweed around it and then, using all his size, strength and weight, tried to pull it over. No matter how much he strained and pulled, the rock would not budge an inch

The Great White Shark tried to push it over. He swam up to the rock as fast as he could and slammed into it as if he were hunting, but to no avail.

The Mako attempted to move it by swimming round and round the rock as fast as it possibly could, hoping to create enough turbulence in the water to tip the rock over. He failed too. The rock would not shift at all.

Then later that same day a very plain and average shaped shark decided to have a try. It had no special size, strength or skill but it had been watching the efforts of the other sharks and thinking it had nothing to lose, set about the task.

Down it swam to the base of the rock and began trying to move the sand away from it. As it moved its head from side to side a small gap slowly appeared beneath the giant stone. The remaining onlookers watched in horror as the rock sank gradually into the hole being created, trapping the sharks head beneath it. The trapped shark started to struggle, shaking its head from side to side then forcefully up and down. It seemed nothing was going to happen but then, applying all its remaining strength in one final effort, heaved as hard as he could. The rock started to tip and suddenly it tumbled over freeing the shark.

The other sharks stared in disbelief. The plain shark who had begun the task hand changed so much! Its head had taken the oddest shape — flattened and wide just like a hammer, with its eyes on the very tips of its new hammer like head (and by the way meant it could now see round corners too)!

So this previously very plain shark had completed the task and passed the test set by Big Blue and earned the right to be named leader and king of the sharks. It had succeeded where others had failed, by sheer effort and determination.

Huge celebrations followed that night. The news of the result of the test was spread throughout the whole ocean. Many plain, unremarkable sharks did what they could to look and be like their king. In fact, some areas of the oceans you can find great schools of Hammerheads — as they came to be known.

The party continued long into the night and as dawn was breaking Big Blue swam by and loudly declared... "Stop, it's Hammer time...."

About the Author

I first came up with the idea of this book in 2009 whilst on a train ride to take a course in scuba diving equipment maintenance when I wrote down the first few characters and first attempt at one of the stories in this book.

After years of toying with different ideas it dawned on me that many of my friends and colleagues and family were having or had young children. This gave me the push to finally put it all down and hopefully get a new generation of people loving the oceans.

So a big thank you goes out to all my family, friends and colleagues children who have been as much of an inspiration as the beautiful underwater world has been in getting me to write this book. I hope you all enjoy it.

Printed in the United States
By Bookmasters